Dedication

For my sweet girl,
You are the light that inspired this story.
Your kindness, joy, and curiosity remind
me daily how precious it is to teach little
hearts with love and grace.
May you always grow in wisdom,
strength, and virtue. Please know how
deeply you are loved.
This is for you, always.

Love,
Mommy

A Note from the Author

"Train up a child in the way he should go, and when he is old he will not depart from it."
—Proverbs 22:6

Tales of Heavenly Manners was born from a longing to plant seeds of virtue in my own daughter's heart—and to help other parents do the same in a gentle, joyful, and memorable way.
In a world that moves fast, I believe we need slow moments of storytelling, rooted in timeless truth and character. Through these books, I hope to nurture kindness, respect, patience, and love in little ones everywhere.

This is the first book in a growing series meant to build up young hearts with Biblical values—one story at a time. Thank you for joining us on this journey.

With grace,
The Little Seed Library

Acknowledgments

This book was written with love and inspired by my sweet daughter. Watching her grow into a kind, curious, and compassionate little girl has been the greatest blessing, and it's her gentle heart that brought this story to life.

Special thanks to the creative tools and technology that helped bring my vision to life.

Thank you to my husband who encouraged me along the way, and to every parent, caregiver, and teacher who understands the importance of raising children with grace, faith, and love.

Most of all, I give thanks to God, the King of all kings, who continues to guide my heart as a mother and reminds me that true royalty begins with a heart that reflects His.

May this book be a reminder to little ones everywhere that good manners, rooted in love and kindness, are the mark of a true princess in God's kingdom. ?

In the Kingdom of Gracewood, there lived a joyful little girl named Princess Lya.

She wore a light blue gown, a golden crown, and always had her favorite book with her. The Book of Heavenly Manners.

Lya loved to read her book each morning. It wasn't just any book. It was filled with God's Word and kind lessons.

"Let all that you do be done in love," she read aloud, smiling.

(1 Corinthians 16:14)

One day, the Queen said, "Lya, kindness is more than reading about it. A real princess shows her heart in how she treats others."
Lya nodded. She wanted to live out her heavenly manners.

First, she visited the royal
kitchen. The baker
dropped her spoon.
"I'll help you, please," said
Lya with a gentle voice.
The baker beamed.
"Thank you, Princess!
You're shining God's love
today!"

Next, Lya walked to the
garden where the
gardener was hard at
work.
"Would you like some
water?" she asked.
"Thank you, my dear," he
said. "That's very thoughtful."
Lya whispered, "Be kind and
compassionate to one
another."

(EPHESIANS 4:32)

A squirrel had stolen crumbs from the picnic basket.
Instead of shouting, Lya said, "He's hungry too. Let's share."
Her friend frowned, but Lya reminded her, "God loves a cheerful giver."

(2 Corinthians 9:7)

That night, Lya knelt beside her bed and prayed:

"Dear Lord, thank You for Your Word. Help me show good manners from the inside out, because I love You."

And from that day forward, everyone in Gracewood knew that the most beautiful thing about Princess Lya was not her crown or her dress...

But her heart that followed Jesus.

Princess Lya's Royal Manners:

- Always say "please" and "thank you"
- Help others whenever you can
- Speak with kindness
- Say sorry and mean it
- Take care of what God has given you
- Pray every day and show love like Jesus

"I PROMISE TO TRY MY BEST TO SHOW ROYAL MANNERS EVERY DAY!"

SIGNED: _____

Dear Sweet Reader,

Thank you for reading my story! I hope it helped you learn how special and important good manners are. God gave us hearts full of kindness-and when we use them, we shine like royalty!
Always remember: you are loved, you are chosen, and you are a child of the King.

With love,
Princess Lya

"Be kind to one another, tenderhearted, forgiving one another, as God in Christ forgave you."
Ephesians 4:32

www.ingramcontent.com/pod-product-compliance
Lightning Source LLC
Chambersburg PA
CBHW040902120626
46551CB00001B/123